Hairy Maclary Scattercat

Lynley Dodd

Hairy Maclary
felt bumptious and bustly,
bossy and bouncy
and frisky and hustly.
He wanted to run.
He wanted to race.
But the MAIN thing he wanted
was something
to
chase.

Greywacke Jones
was hunting a bee.

BUT ALONG CAME HAIRY MACLARY. . .

and chased her up high
in the sycamore tree.

Butterball Brown
was washing a paw.

BUT ALONG CAME HAIRY MACLARY. . .

and bustled him under
a rickety door.

Pimpernel Pugh
was patting a ball.

BUT ALONG CAME HAIRY MACLARY. . .

and chased her away
over Pemberton's wall.

Slinky Malinki
was down in the reeds.

BUT ALONG CAME HAIRY MACLARY. . .

and hustled him into
a drum full of weeds.

Mushroom Magee
was asleep on a ledge.

BUT ALONG CAME HAIRY MACLARY. . .

and chased her away
through a hole in the hedge.

Down on the path
by an old wooden rail,
twitching a bit,
was the tip of a tail.
With a bellicose bark
and a boisterous bounce,
Hairy Maclary
was ready
to
POUNCE

BUT AROUND CAME SCARFACE CLAW...

who bothered
and bustled him,
rustled and hustled him,
raced him
and chased him

ALL the way
home.

Books by Lynley Dodd

First published in 1985 by Mallinson Rendel Publishers Ltd.
Reprinted 1985, 1986, 1988, 1990, 1992, 2000, 2001, 2007
This edition published by Penguin Group (NZ), 2012.

© Lynley Dodd, 1985

ISBN 978-0-14350532-7

Type set by Challis Datacom, Wellington, New Zealand.
Printed in China through Colorcraft Ltd., Hong Kong